A New Beginning

Willow J Wolfe

Published by Willow J Wolfe, 2023.

A NEW BEGINNING

First edition. August 5, 2023.

ISBN: 979-8223666639

Written by Willow J Wolfe.

Table of Contents

A New Beginning

By
Willow J Wolfe

Chapter One

"Hold tight there lads!"

The water around them surged and swelled violently, tossing the men below around easily as they fought in vain to control the ship. Kay laughed from her place high in the rigging, her long dark hair dancing around her in the wind as she looked to the horizon. The storm brewed ever closer; she loved the way the wind whipped around her with an untamed energy she could feel all the way down to her toes, as if to remind everyone they were merely visitors in its wild domain.

The captain shouted at her from the deck and she sighed, realizing it was time to get down. One of these days she was going to find a captain brave enough to teach her to sail, but she supposed she should be grateful he had allowed her aboard in the first place. This expedition to the New World had seemed the perfect chance to prove herself – even if the leader of the explorers, a man called John Smith, thought her merely the entertainment.

The crew leapt out of her way as she slowly made her way down the rigging and she chuckled. "Silly superstitious fools." She probably shouldn't complain though. Those very superstitions were probably the only things keeping her safe. There was no mistaking the hunger on their faces as they watched her from a distance. Being the only female on board definitely had its drawbacks and with that in mind, she allowed the captain to usher her below deck, running her fingers over the notches in her traveling stick as she went.

It had been her father's idea. Before leaving on any trip, they would craft a new walking stick and etch their destination on the top. That way, not only would the stick provide a means of protection and help them keep track of the time, when they came home it was a nice reminder of their trip. By her calculations, they should be reaching the new world soon. Her soul itched with excitement. An entire new world to explore. Leagues of uncharted wilderness just waiting to be discovered, and she was getting to experience it for herself.

She knew her life was unique. Her father, a loving man with a thirst for exploration rivaled only by her own, had never seemed to care his only child was a girl – nor had he seemed to care how society thought she should act. Her mother had objected at first, spending endless hours attempting to pull Kay inside and force her to be still. But then, her mother had gotten sick, and seeing the apathy creeping onto her daughter's face, had urged her to follow her own path and never let anyone convince her otherwise.

Their relatives and neighbors were a different story, constantly chastising her father for allowing Kay to act as she pleased. They felt he had shattered any hope she might have of finding a nice husband, and often snatched her away to their homes for "proper lessons." They would force her into a ridiculous dress and scold her for speaking out of turn. Her father never failed to rescue her though, and when they got home, he'd teach her something new of his trade. Where most girls learned how to cook and care for a house, she learned how to make arrows and how to spot animal tracks.

Now, at the age of twenty-three, she was one of the best trackers in the country. Her tall slim body gave her an advantage, allowing her to discover smaller hidden gems that bulkier men might miss. She spent more time atop high forest trees than inside her own home. She knew there were few trackers who could rival her, even if most men laughed at and dismissed her skills. This time it would be different. This time she was alone. They wouldn't be unable to deny her this time, and for that, she would endure all the taunts and jeers of the crew.

She listened as the storm raged and decided that now would be as good a time as any to replenish her food stores. Her father might have had enough influence to charter her passage, but once at sea, she was on her own. Anything that went wrong – including this storm – was apparently her fault, and the men spared no chance to tell her so. The cook was especially vicious, thinking her barely worthy of table scraps. Kay had quickly learned to snatch food and hide it away in her little cubby hole whenever she had the chance. Poking her head around the corner, she quickly ensured the cook was still in his bailing position near one of the portholes, before sneaking through the ship's innards to the kitchen.

Near dawn, the storm abated, and the clear rain-freshened air revealed that Kay need not have bothered with the food at all. At first she thought something must be wrong, waking up to a cacophonous roar of men shouting from above. She'd frantically rushed to the deck, and she felt her heart flutter as she caught her first sight of the new world. She climbed into the rigging for a better look, her eyes greedily scanning in the approaching land mass. She couldn't believe it. She was here. She had finally escaped all those silly ideas that women were to be seen and not heard, as if they were mere objects. Her heart began to race as she tried to guess what awaited her on the shore. Technically she had been brought on this trip as a member of John Smith's team, but she knew he had no intention of letting her participate in the actual work. Her father had convinced him to bring her along, but that was the extent of his cooperation.

Once on shore, she dutifully waited for her orders for almost an hour before shouldering her pack and setting out into the dense foliage surrounding the riverbed. The forest was amazing. Everywhere she looked, something new waited to be discovered. She kept an eye out for a suitable place to camp where she would be safe from any elements or uninvited visitors, finally spying what looked like a natural path heading up the side of a cliff. She hiked her way up, pleased to discover a small alcove about thirty feet up which overlooked the river.

It was almost too perfect. There was plenty of room to build a fire and set up camp, and she could also see the ship fairly well over the trees. Setting down her pack, she pulled out her journal and recorded her exact location. She then emptied the contents of her pack completely so she could take stock of what she still needed. She'd left most of her food on the ship so that would definitely need replenishing. She placed her flint and other cooking supplies near the edge, figuring she'd sleep against the wall. After that, all that remained were the few tools she'd brought to help her gather supplies such as her knife and traps.

"First things first," she said as she placed her tools back in her pack. "Water."

She hoped to find a water source other than the river. After all, she would like to bathe at some point and there was no telling how far up the river the men would venture. She wandered through the foliage, being sure to keep a close eye on her surroundings as she traveled further into the forest. She didn't have to hike far before she found an area with a denser underbrush, a sure sign of a nearby water source. Easing her way through the brambles, Kay was pleased to find a small pool attached to a spring on the other side.

She refilled her canteen and briefly washed her clothes, hanging them in the nearby trees to air dry before carefully and gingerly slipping into the water, gasping as its cold caress sent shivers of goose bumps roving across her body. Lying back, she allowed her body to relax as she contemplated her next moves. The rest of the day would have to be spent gathering supplies. She needed firewood, food, and something to defend herself with.

For what seemed like the millionth time, she wished she had her bow. The captain had flat out refused to allow her aboard with it, and she still seethed at the thought. She'd been outraged when he'd strode straight past her on the dock and demanded her father remove the weapon. She'd been determined to keep it, but her father had shaken his head and solemnly held out his hand to take it from her, much to her dismay. Her bow was one of her most prized possessions. It was made of yew and had been stained a dark cherry color that contrasted perfectly with the green leaves etched and painted into the front. Her father had given it to her years before in celebration of her first tracking expedition. Now, a stranger in a foreign world, she longed for the comfort of her bow. She still had her lacquered dagger – another gift from her father – but it didn't give her the same feeling.

I suppose I could always make one. She thought to herself. *But that will take a few days at least and I really want something now.*

Half an hour later, she reluctantly exited the spring and retrieved her damp clothing. She made her way back to camp, checking her rabbit traps as she went, but they were empty.

"Damn. Is it too much to ask for a bit of fresh meat?"

Spotting some berries, she sighed, knowing they would have to do for now and pulled a simple cloth bag from within her pack, gathering enough to last her a day or so. Her stomach grumbled in protest, and she resolved herself to sneaking back onto the ship to steal whatever supplies she needed. She couldn't hunt until she had a bow. As much as she didn't want to return to the ship, it was her best shot.

She wandered towards her camp, trying to spot any additional spots that would be well suited for a trap, but as she turned towards a small clearing, she stopped dead. There was a man in front of her. His eyes were focused towards the ship; apparently he hadn't noticed her. She drew a breath, intending to call out to him, but stopped herself at the last moment, unwilling to add yet another enemy to her list. He was definitely not from the ship. She would have remembered seeing someone so gorgeous amid all the ruffians. His features were sharp, and appeared almost feminine save for the branching tattoo on his cheek that extended down past his collarbone. His long hair was white and billowed around him like water. His very being seemed to exude a feel of airy wildness – even his clothes danced around him. He turned slightly and she ducked back behind a tree to avoid being seen.

It's like he's not even human, she thought as he knelt to inspect something. She crept around the tree, trying to see what he was looking at, but she'd barely made a step before his head flicked towards her. His dark eyes locked with hers for a split second before he leapt into the air, vanishing among the trees. She ran forward, but he was gone.

Chapter Two

Sehouma observed the young woman carefully. She didn't appear dangerous, but then, most sleeping animals didn't. Her presence confused him. When she'd spotted him earlier, he'd followed her back to her base, amused with her vain attempts to locate him. She'd clearly been trained as a hunter. She moved deliberately, barely a twig scrapped with her movements. But as her movements became increasingly cautious, he had to wonder who she was hiding from. Logic stated she must have come with the other visitors, however while they exuded greed and arrogance, her aura appeared merely curious. But if she had come with them, why was no one searching for her? And why was she so determined to remain hidden?

In the past, whenever humans had entered his forest, the women had typically stayed within the camp, tending to the children while the men scouted. This girl however seemed almost fearful of the other visitors. He could sense no danger from her though; clearly the woman was a being all her own. Deciding to observe her a while longer, he built up her dying fire and retreated to the trees to find a good vantage point to watch her and the other visitors.

Chapter Three

When Kay awoke, she was surprised to find her fire crackling away merrily, as if she'd merely closed her eyes for a minute, but the sky was dark, the sun long set. Shrugging it off, she gathered her tools and looked out over the river, trying to determine the best route to approach the ship. As far as she could tell, they hadn't spread out too much, which worked well for her. The less ground she had to cover, the less chance she'd get caught.

She slipped silently through the trees to the edge of the forest, deciding to approach the camp from the side. She could see every inch of the base in perfect detail now. The sheer lack of effort being put towards constructing the camp astounded her. She vividly remembered hearing the men boast they wouldn't rest until they'd harvested enough timber to wall in their entire base. As far as she could tell, they hadn't even completed a third of it yet.

I guess I should be thankful though. She thought as she studied the camp. *I doubt I'd have been able to scale a wall.*

There weren't too many men out. They'd mostly all gone to sleep save for the few guards pacing the perimeter. She watched them for a moment, huffing quietly in annoyance as she realized they seemed to be smarter than she'd given them credit for. Their strategic pacing left little opening to sneak in. She really didn't want to charge in blindly – especially since she wasn't entirely sure she was welcome. Glancing onto the ship, she smiled as she noticed the practically deserted deck.

I'll bet there are still plenty of supplies left on board.

Stealing down to the water, Kay quietly slipped into the river and swam out to the far side of the ship. "This is completely ridiculous," she muttered as she searched for handholds to pull herself up. It would be so much easier if she could just walk into camp like any other member of the team, but she couldn't stand their eyes upon her. She knew what those men wanted from her, and while their fearless leader had ordered them to leave her alone, she didn't want to push the matter. She finally reached the deck and peeked her head slowly over the railing – just as a sailor walked past her. Ducking down, she cursed her luck.

That was close.

When no one else appeared, she lifted herself over the railing, keeping low to the deck as she sidled over to the cargo hold. She inched the hatch open, cringing when it squeaked, and dropped delicately to the room below. She'd been right. At least half the cargo was still onboard. She found the armory first, picking up an old recurve bow, complete with quiver and arrows, leaned against the back wall. She took it, as well as a pistol and ammo pouch. "Ok, now I just need a blanket," she whispered, turning towards the bunks. On the way, she picked up a first aid kit and a small mallet she found lying on top of a crate, ignoring the small voice in her mind that reminded her things never went this well for her. All she needed was five more minutes and she'd be safely on her way home.

Chapter Four

Sehouma watched the young girl with rapt curiosity. Her obvious attempts at secrecy confirmed his suspicions. The men were not her allies. He chuckled as she had to duck down to avoid being seen by a passing guard. A moment later, she disappeared below deck, just in time too. The noise of the hatch opening had drawn the attention of another guard who ran back to investigate.

It was some time before she reappeared, laden with supplies. He watched as she carefully closed the hatch to avoid making any further noises. But then, she appeared to hesitate, as if she hadn't thought about how she was going to escape. She moved to the far side of the ship and carefully began to lower one of the ship's smaller vessels into the water.

She'll be too late. He thought, sensing more men below decks approaching the hatch. He watched as she continued, unaware that she was about to have company. The hatch opened and her face contorted in fear. He wondered why she feared them so. Hadn't she come here on the same vessel? Whatever the reason, he felt something pull him to save her, but if he went now, he was sure to be seen.

I should have gone to retrieve her immediately.

She was desperately trying to get the boat down, but the men were already appearing from below. They laughed, apparently in deep conversation and as they turned towards the camp, Sehouma saw his chance. He leapt to the ship, landing directly in front of her. She opened her mouth to scream but he quickly silenced her with a hand over her mouth. Before she knew what was happening, he had stepped behind her and gracefully picked her up as one of the men turned around.

"Intruders!"

The man drew his pistol, but Sehouma was already gone, a smirk on his face as he sped through the night sky. He landed on the riverbank some distance from the ship and gently set Kay down.

"How did...who?" she rambled, her eyes flickering quickly all over his face.

He looked her over carefully. Her language was strange, unlike any he had heard before. He wanted to learn more, and swirled his spirit around them, cloaking them in its power. The water stirred beside them, disrupted by the energy as he touched her mind with his own. Confusion and fear once again crept into her features and he quickly retreated.

"My name is Sehouma," he said awkwardly.

"You speak English?" She asked, her eyes widening in shock.

He nodded. "For now. What is your name?"

"Uh....it's Kay. I'm sorry, but who are you? How the hell did you jump like that? It was like you flew!"

"It doesn't matter. Who are you? Why were you sneaking and who are those men?"

She crossed her arms over her chest, hesitation plain in her voice. "Why should I answer your questions if you don't want to answer mine?" She glared at him for a few moments and he watched, unsure how to proceed. She made a valid point, but he needed answers and he didn't know how else to go about getting them. "They are settlers," she said finally, surprising him with her response. Touching her spirit with his own may allow him to speak her language but that didn't mean he understood everything.

"What does that mean?"

"It means they're planning to live here. They'll build a base and expand wherever they can. I however, am merely an explorer. I just want to see everything this land has to offer. Now I think I've been patient enough. I answered your questions. Now you answer mine. Who are you? You can't be human."

"No," he chuckled. "I am not human. I'm not sure how to explain in terms you'd understand. I mean you no harm though."

"Nor I you. But I um...really should get back to my camp. Thank you for helping me," she said, blushing and bowing slightly as she backed away.

He watched her go, his mind reeling from their brief encounter. She was unlike any human he'd encountered before. They normally sought to exploit others to achieve their own desires, but this woman merely sought knowledge. From what he could see, she wanted to explore and understand as much as she could. In that way, she reminded him a great deal of himself. He had always considered himself a curious being and from the looks of it, her curiosity might very well rival his own. He needed more information, but he'd spent far too much time watching her as it was. He had other duties to attend to.

Chapter Five

Kay grumbled as she ate her breakfast. "I feel as if I've just fallen into the river!" She wiped her brow and pulled her hair up off her neck, tying it with a bit of string. "I had hoped I might escape this damned humidity when I left England, but it's just as bad here!"

Her flesh burned and she longed to scratch it, but knew that would only make matters worse. She didn't want to tear her skin anymore than she already had, and once she started scratching, she doubted she'd be able to stop.

She'd had this problem since she was a child. Anytime the weather was humid, her skin became increasingly red and itchy. Her body bore scars from her younger years, before she'd known the damage she was doing to herself. Even now, after she'd learned to avoid touching the welts as much as possible, there were still times – such as when she slept – that she couldn't resist.

This morning, she'd woken to find blood under her fingernails and she'd groaned when she saw the blood on her blanket. The backs of her knees were bloody and raw, as were the insides of her elbows and several areas on her neck. Normally, she applied a salve to both relieve and prevent these breakouts, but she'd long run out. She'd decided to spend the morning indulging in a long soak to soothe some of the pain. A dip in the ocean would help even more, but Kay knew from experience that the pain would be more than she could handle. The salty spray of the sea on the ship had been bad enough. She didn't even want to think about submerging her entire body.

She reached the spring and gently waded into the pool, sighing happily as the cool water caressed her. As much as it pained her skin, water had always calmed her. As a child, her first expedition had been to find the waterfall her mother had claimed was nearby. It had then become one of her favorite hideaways. She'd even made a clubhouse of sorts in a cave near the base, loving the sound of the water crashing all around her as she imagined she was mapping out unknown worlds far from home.

Sliding further into the spring, she hissed as the water hit her torn flesh. It hurt, but she tried to ignore it, knowing she'd feel better in the long run. However, she couldn't help the yelp that escaped her as her knees touched the surface.

"Damn it all!" she bellowed, diving underwater to get it over with. She emerged with a shriek, cursing her skin as it continued to burn.

"Are you alright?"

Kay screamed, crashed into the water and cautiously turned around, relaxing slightly when she saw Sehouma standing at the edge of the spring. "Oh thank God!" She murmured. He looked at her curiously and she tried to explain. "I was afraid you were one of the men from the ship."

"Ah," he said, nodding briefly. "Why were you shouting?"

"My skin," Kay said, pointing to the blisters on her neck. "The humidity makes it itch incessantly. I was hoping to soothe it by soaking for a while, but the water burns."

"I see."

He disappeared into the trees and Kay shrugged, sinking underwater to cool her face. She wondered why she wasn't afraid of Sehouma. She hadn't been lying when she said she was afraid of the men on the ship, so why wasn't she afraid of him as well? She knew basically nothing about him, except that he wasn't human – and that knowledge alone should have terrified her. So why didn't it?

Sighing, she lay back to watch the clouds. It looked like it might rain; she hoped it wouldn't though. She wanted to explore and she really needed to go hunting. There were only so many berries a person could eat without wishing to never lay eyes on one again...and she was definitely past that point.

She stayed in the spring for almost an hour before forcing herself out, knowing that would have to do for now. Her skin still hurt, but the pain had dulled significantly. She could only hope daily soaks would keep it under control. She refilled her canteen and ventured off, keeping an eye out for branches she could fashion arrows from. She also kept an eye out for any scouts from the camp, but they seemed to still be focused on their silly fortress.

She also wondered why she hadn't seen any natives – unless you counted Sehouma. She knew there were natives in this new world. She'd heard other explorers discussing them with her father, so she was surprised they hadn't run into them yet. However, Sehouma might also be responsible for their absence – a thought which only slightly disturbed her. She continued deeper into the forest, marveling at its density as the underbrush began clinging to her with every step.

"I'm beginning to think this forest doesn't want to be explored."

Chapter Six

Sehouma watched through the trees as the girl snagged her hair on a particularly thorny bush. He chuckled as she cursed vehemently, violently freeing herself before clambering into a nearby birch tree, apparently deciding that the trees were better means of travel. She was definitely a mystery and he found himself watching her more and more as time went on, attempting to learn whatever he could about her. He wondered why she'd come here. Surely any family she might have would be worried for her survival. Although, as she calmly shot a rabbit and dropped gracefully from the tree to retrieve it, he had to admit she had no problems taking care of herself.

He reluctantly returned his gaze to the ship and the men scrambling around it. They had more than two thirds of their camp walled in now, and a small group seemed to be preparing a scouting mission. He sighed. He would have to follow them – even though he would much rather follow the high spirited Kay who he could still hear cursing the very trees that held her. They couldn't be allowed to disturb the forest any more than they already had. He needed to learn as much as he could about them before he could discern how to force them to leave. He somehow doubted they would be as easy to remove as the natives.

He watched as their arrogant leader began shouting out orders and passing out some sort of dark, shiny staves to the men. The men were joking about something, barks of laughter escaping some of them as others made strange expressions and cowered before them. He wondered what those staves were. They didn't look like anything he'd ever encountered, but the way the men were wielding them, he doubted they were good. He'd have to ask Kay later.

The men fanned out into the forest, making little effort to conceal their presence. Sehouma hesitated, unsure which men to follow. He did not want them to stumble across the young girl or her camp, but at the same time, he had a forest to protect. As two of the men trailed off towards the west, he knew what he had to do. Whistling softly, he held out his hand and waited for a small bird to land before speaking several short chirps.

The bird tweeted softly at him and then flew off once again, this time in the direction the girl had gone. He listened for a moment as the bird conveyed his message to others who began fanning out into the forest after the other men. Content his friends would warn him should the men venture too far, Sehouma followed the remaining two men, hoping they would tire quickly and turn back before he was forced to act.

Chapter Seven

Kay scoffed, watching the sailors celebrate the completion of their base. When she'd returned to her camp an hour earlier, they'd been putting up the final pieces of the wall, but she didn't understand their logic. The wall only extended to the water's edge, meaning anyone who wanted in could just swim around the wall. But then again, she had to remind herself who had built said wall. *They're so pigheaded they're probably assuming the "savages" won't be smart enough to swim.* She couldn't help the look of disgust that swept over her at that thought; anyone who drank endlessly and constantly tried to beat each other senseless as these men did had little right to call someone else "savage".

Shrugging, she stoked the fire and began to prepare for bed, frowning when she spotted a wooden cup near her bedroll. Picking it up she realized it was a paste of some kind and gave it a cautious sniff. It smelled pleasant enough, whatever it was, but she had no idea where it came from. It hadn't been there that morning, of that she was sure. But when she thought about it, there was really only one possibility. *Sehouma. He must have left it here...but why?* She gave the cup another curious sniff.

"It's for your skin," His voice called out from behind her and she jerked, almost dropping the cup as she spun to face him.

"Stop doing that!" She hissed, hand clasped to her fluttering heart. "You'll kill me!"

"Apologies," he said regally, bowing slightly.

"It's ok," Kay said, baffling at the slight flush she felt creeping up her skin as she walked back to the fire. "I was just about to prepare some tea, would you like to join me?" He nodded and she filled her small kettle and set it by the fire to warm, wishing she had a spit to hang it on. "So, what did you say this was?"

"It's a salve for your skin," he said, sitting down on the other side of the fire. "It should help with the pain."

"Oh," Kay said, picking up the cup again. Scooping a small amount onto her fingers, she spread it gingerly onto her elbow, surprised by how cool it felt. It burned slightly as the paste was absorbed into her flesh, but soon her skin quieted and the desire to scratch slowly faded into nothingness. It felt amazing. Looking back to Sehouma, she was overcome with an intense desire to thank him somehow, but this only reminded her she knew almost nothing about him. She wondered if he had a family, or even where he came from. He was watching her intently and she couldn't help but wonder if he was thinking similar thoughts about her.

"So," she said, trying to break the silence. "Do you mind if I ask you something?"

"Only if I may ask you something as well," he replied, his eyes gleaming mischievously.

Kay shrugged, "It's only fair." He nodded in agreement and Kay tried to think what to ask first. Deciding on the most obvious, she said softly. "So, I know you said you're not human...are you a demon?"

He chuckled and the deep sound echoed around her camp; Kay shivered.

"No, I'm not a demon." He turned to look out over the forest and Kay wondered if that's all he was willing to say on the matter, but then, just as she was about to ask him what he wanted to know, he spoke again. "It's difficult to convey what I am in a way you would understand. I am neither human, demon, or god. I supposed you could call me an in-between."

"What do you mean?"

"I am the protector of this forest."

She frowned, scoffing as she thought to herself. *Yeah, that definitely answers that.*

Forgetting that he was supposed to be asking her something now, Kay sat up a little straighter and voiced the question burning inside her mind. "How can you speak English?" She was trying very hard to hide her shock at his knowledge of her language. It just didn't seem possible for him to speak English if he was the only person in this forest. She had thought at first that maybe he was a survivor from a shipwreck at some point, but clearly that was not the case. He talked as if he'd always been here.

"So many questions," he chuckled. "I allowed my spirit to briefly touch yours when we first met. It forms a connection which allows me to talk in whatever language you speak. It's the same way I talk to the animals."

"Oh," she said, absentmindedly dabbing a bit more salve onto her knees. "I guess that makes sense."

"Where do you come from?"

"Far away, across the ocean, in England and it's probably as different from this forest as it can be. Everything there is loud and overbearing. I much prefer it here."

"Really?" he replied, genuine surprise resonating in his voice.

She nodded, and he was slightly surprised to hear her scoff. "Oh yes, everyone at home is too interested in trying to make me into something I'm not. Always pushing me to act how they think I should, not caring for my own dreams and desires. It's suffocating. I'd much rather stay here where I'm able to live freely."

"I see."

They sat in companionable silence for a moment as Kay tried to work up the courage to speak again. She wanted to know about his family. Surely he had to have one. Everyone had a family, even if they wished they didn't.

"What of your family?" he blurted suddenly. "Don't you miss them?"

There was a sadness to his voice that pulled at her heart. So he did have a family, but where were they? Why was he alone? He gazed at her expectantly and she remembered he'd asked her a question. "My father is an explorer himself. He taught me everything I know. My mother died when I was young."

He nodded solemnly, his gaze dropping to the ground.

"What about your family?" she murmured, half afraid of what she'd hear. But before he could answer, a sparrow flitted into the camp and landed on his hand. She watched as the bird chirped avidly at Sehouma, and he nodded, his expression darkening the longer he listened.

"Apologies," he said, getting to his feet. "This one is needed elsewhere."

He was almost out of sight before Kay realized what was happening. She made to follow him, but he was gone, without even a scrape of leaves to give him away.

Chapter Eight

Sehouma's feet barely touched the tops of the trees as he sped towards the Elder Tree. He'd been afraid of this. He'd been able to distract the men earlier by leading them on a hunt through the forest until he'd circled them back around to their base, but now they were back. He had to keep them from damaging it. No matter what, he had to keep the Elder safe. He slowed his steps as the sailors' voices became clear.

"Come on, there's nothing here. Let's go back to camp. I'm hungry."

"Our orders were to search this whole area, we're staying."

"I still don't even know why we're bothering," the shorter of the two men said, snapping a nearby sapling as he trampled through the undergrowth. "Will's a drunk. How do we know he didn't imagine the savage with that stupid girl? He's the only one that saw them, and there's no way they could have gotten off the ship without being seen."

"Maybe, but we still have to check. Come on."

The men continued their trek, venturing further and further into the forest, unaware that high above them, Sehouma was cracking his knuckles. He didn't want to kill them, but if they went much further, he'd have no choice. The very forest itself depended on the safety of the Elder. He couldn't allow anything to happen to it.

Turn around, he silently begged as the two men continued to argue. *Give up. Now.*

But they were still walking and Sehouma reluctantly readied himself to strike. He dropped silently to the ground and slowly edged towards the two men, hating himself for what he was about to do. But then, angry voices echoed from the direction of the ship and he paused. Something was happening. A moment later an explosion shook the forest and he leapt back into the trees as the men turned towards the sound.

"What the devil?" the shorter man said, stupidly trying to squint enough to see through the trees. "Did that?"

"Come on!"

They took off and Sehouma released a sigh of relief. The Elder was safe. Glancing over the trees, he noted smoke rising from the ship and the cacophonous voices echoing through the trees.

I wonder what's happened.

Chapter Nine

Kay watched the men flail about their smoldering ship, clearly oblivious about what to do. She'd been awoken by the explosion and had momentarily debated going to help, but this was better. She only wished she could hear them hurl insults at each other as they ran around, all willy nilly. From what she could tell something on the shore – one of the barrels of black powder by the looks of it – had exploded and the debris had caught on the ships sails.

"What was that?"

She jumped; would he ever stop sneaking up on her? "An explosion." His eyebrow quirked in confusion and she motioned to the ledge where she stood, waiting for him to join her before pointing towards the ship. "See those barrels they're rolling away to the edge of the forest? The powder inside them is extremely volatile and highly flammable. So, they're rolling them away to keep another from exploding."

"I see," he said softly, but his expression remained one of utter bewilderment. "How did it happen?"

"Not sure, but I think that man is to blame considering how everyone is shouting at him."

He watched the men for a moment, his eyes wide with wonder as he watched them restore order.

"Thank you again for the salve," she blurted suddenly. "My skin hasn't felt this good in years." He nodded and she walked to where her bedroll lay propped next to the wall. "So, what was the hurry earlier? You disappeared so fast, something awful must have happened."

Sehouma contemplated her for a moment, unsure if he should trust her or not. His previous experience with humans told him that he should lie, but something told him she was different. She was no danger to the Elder Tree. Maybe it would be nice to have someone to confide in for once. He'd been alone for so long, and her aura was soothing. Glancing out over the forest, he decided to take a chance.

"There is a tree in this forest that I must protect," he said, watching her carefully to gauge her reaction. "It gives life to the forest. I must ensure its survival."

"Wow. That must be some tree. What about family? Don't you ever get lonely?"

His lips rose in a sad smile as he gazed out over the forest. "Not really. I have the animals to talk to. And even without them, it's not so bad. At least I'm free. The truth is, I am not so different from you. My home is filled with rules, and in order to escape them, I came here."

"Yeah, I guess so," She thought about the similarity of their situations. He seemed to value his freedom as much as she did, but she wasn't sure she would go to the extent that he had. She missed her father. Could she really give him up forever just to escape the rules of home? Already she could feel the twinges of homesickness edging into her bones. She was loving this experience, but could she really do this forever?

She tried unsuccessfully to hide a yawn, frowning when he stood suddenly. "I'm keeping you awake. I'll go."

"No! It's alright, you don't have to go," she exclaimed, reaching her hand out to him even as another yawn engulfed her.

He chuckled. "Good night Kay."

Chapter Ten

"The water looks perfect today," Kay murmured, staring longingly through the trees towards the ocean. The continued use of Sehouma's salve over the past week had done wonders and when she'd woken that morning, her skin had been clearer than it had in years. She'd been hard pressed not to straight for the ocean. It had been so long; she barely even remembered the feel of the ocean on her skin, but logic dictated first she needed to finish restocking her camp. She still needed to make some arrows, and her water supply was running dangerously low. No, first she would have to go check her traps and visit the spring. Maybe later she could explore a little further down the coast and find a good spot to swim. She could probably even get some fishing in, if she could fashion a spear of some kind.

She walked casually, enjoying the sounds of the morning as birds twittered above her and squirrels darted from tree to tree. Once again, she found herself marveling at what a magical place they had happened upon. She had the feeling anything was possible in these woods. Remembering what Sehouma had said about the Elder Tree, she wondered if all the animals had sensed the tree and that's what led them here. She couldn't deny that the forest seemed to exude a sense of safety. She wished her father was here to see this, knowing he would appreciate the serenity of the forest as well, but he was worlds away. She'd originally intended to send a letter home with the captain whenever the ship returned to England for supplies, but somehow she doubted that would be possible.

A man's voice rang out suddenly and Kay jerked out of her thoughts, ducking behind a tree as two of the men came into view.

"What's this?"

"What's it look like you ninny? It's a trap!"

"I know that," the man replied and Kay could practically hear his teeth grinding together in anger. "I meant, who the blazes put it here?"

"Who knows? Maybe that girl put it there. There's a spring nearby; she could be using it as her water source."

"That silly woman? She's too stupid to know how to hunt."

"True. Guess it was the savages then."

Kay swore under her breath as one of the men knelt down and stole the rabbit from her trap. She didn't know what to do. She still had several more traps in this area and if she waited, they might leave without discovering them. On the other hand though, she really didn't want them to find her either.

"Surprised we haven't seen them yet."

"Well, if you count Will's story."

"Yeah, but I don't count his story. That man will drink himself into believing the Queen's here before long."

The other man laughed and they turned to leave the clearing, walking straight towards her. Panicking, she leapt into the tree, trying to remain as silent as possible as she hurriedly climbed out of sight. She stopped about a third of the way up, intending to wait for them to pass so she could then proceed with her day. However, just as they reached her, she felt the branch she perched upon creak ominously.

Looking down, she realized that in her rush to remain undetected, she'd stopped on a rotting limb – and it was cracking. She swore, reaching for the branch above her, but too late. The limb snapped and she screamed, feeling her world dissolve into pain, her arm smacking audibly into a branch as she fell.

Chapter Eleven

Sehouma stood in front of the Elder, his arm pressed to the trunk almost reverently. There had been too many close calls. He was quickly running out of options. It was only a matter of time before he'd be forced to act. In all the years he'd been here, he'd never encountered a situation like this, and he was somewhat baffled on how to handle it without major bloodshed. In the past, the humans who'd come here had been merely passing through and hadn't ever attempted to set up a permanent base, but something told him these men were different. If he did anything to them, more would inevitably follow to seek them out, if they weren't already. Kay had said they were planning to set up permanent residence here, which probably meant more were already on their way and then then he would have even more problems. All paths seemed to lead to war, and he had absolutely no idea how to prevent it.

When he'd originally volunteered to come here, he never would have guessed something like this would happen. The forest was so dense, he assumed no one would ever find it. However, every year there seemed to be more and more humans that wandered into the forest, each more curious than the rest. He sometimes wondered if he should go home and ask for help, but he couldn't leave the forest unprotected. Especially now.

He smiled as he realized part of the reason he refused to leave was he didn't want to end his time with Kay. She was quickly becoming an integral part of his life. Animals were nice to talk to, but they didn't ease his loneliness. Over the past week, he'd spent every moment he could with Kay and it seemed his feelings were reciprocated. Twice he'd found her searching the forest for him, although she'd denied it, claiming she merely wanted to explore. The curious gleam in her eyes was unmistakable though. He knew she wanted to know more about where he came from, and more than once, he'd almost told her. However, he couldn't shake the idea that once she knew, she might leave to go search for his home, which was miles away. Then he'd never get to see her and he had no doubts his loneliness would only be worse for it.

A shifting in the wind pulled him from his thoughts and he turned towards the encampments. Something was happening. He frowned, his hand falling to his side as the birds began to shriek in earnest. *What's going on?*

And then he heard her scream.

Chapter Twelve

Kay groaned, aware that she was curled on the ground. Her arm felt completely shattered; she could feel shards of bone gouging into her muscles with a gleeful vengeance. She thought someone was above her, but couldn't bring herself to care. She wanted to die. At least then the pain would stop. Something was pushing against her side and she became aware of another presence beside her. Opening one bleary eye, she saw the two men, glaring down at her as one of them nudged her side with his boot.

"Awake are you?" He said gruffly. "What the hell were you doing in that tree?"

"Trying to steal from us no doubt," said the other, kicking some dirt towards her face. "We don't have any food, wench."

"Serves you right," said the first, kneeling beside her. "We've been looking for you. See, lots of the men back at camp need looking after; and you're the only one that can help." He reached out and touched her broken arm, Kay tried to squirm away, but her arm twisted and she shrieked. The man apparently liked this and pulled her towards him just to hear her scream again.

"Haha, I'm going to enjoy this. My wife wasn't too fun even when I was home, so it's been a while."

He straddled her and Kay began to sob. It was too much. Her friends had warned her. They tried to tell her how dangerous it would be. She'd been too determined to prove her skills to listen though, and now she was going to pay for it.

She felt the cloth of her shirt rip away and felt cool air on her skin. He reached for her pants, but stopped as the air filled with a snarling such as she'd never heard. The man's weight left her and she heard a massive thud as something heavy hit the tree. She groaned, panicking as she felt hands upon her and someone lifted her into the air. She struggled, but the arms that held her were gentle. She opened her eyes, and through her blurred vision, she thought saw a gleam of silver hair and heard Sehouma's voice; then all went dark.

Chapter Thirteen

Sehouma looked down at the girl, trying to decide what to do. She needed help. That much was certain. However, while he could set her bones and give her herbs for the pain, the healing process would be long and hard. For the first time in years, he thought of his father and the healing powers he possessed. He could heal her instantly. The problem was his father was at least a two day's run from here. Could he risk leaving the tree that long? It was only a matter of time before the men began searching for him in earnest. He just hadn't been able to control himself. He'd seen the man atop her, laughing as he tore her clothing, and before he'd known what he was doing, he'd thrown the offending male into a tree and had relished feeling the life drain from him upon impact. The other human had bolted, and if Kay hadn't groaned in pain, he probably would have chased him down as well.

She groaned again, shifting slightly in his arms and Sehouma made his decision. The tree would have to fend for itself now. The animals knew to help, and hopefully he would be able to get someone to come keep watch in his absence. He couldn't let her suffer. Searching the clearing, he found some herbs and a few pieces of bark and used those to fashion a splint. She shrieked as he set her arm, but remained unconscious as he carried her back to her camp and laid her down in her bedding to rest while he gathered what was needed for the journey. When he returned, he quickly packed up everything in her meager camp and strapped everything to his back, picking her up and settling her gently into the crook of his arm.

She was so fragile. He couldn't get the thought out of his head. If he pressed his fingers against her, she would break. He hadn't wanted to admit how much this frail creature had come to mean to him, but when he'd heard her scream... He refused to think what might have happened if he had been out of earshot. Now all he could do was place his faith in his own two feet and hope that his father would see it within himself to heal her, even though Sehouma knew he would be furious with him for leaving his post.

The forest seemed to part around him, as if all within could sense the importance of this journey. Midway through the day, the young girl shifted in his arms, moaning softly, and he slowed to a stop beside a river. *The herbs must be wearing off.* Settling her down gently, he gathered some water and then set about making a poultice to place beneath her splint. It wasn't as effective as if she had eaten it, but it would at least take the edge off her pain so she could sleep. She really needed to drink some water as well, but he couldn't bring himself to wake her. Even in sleep, her aura exuded fear. He didn't want to pull her back into consciousness to suffer more.

By the end of the second day, he was so tired he barely acknowledged the ground beneath his feet. All thought had slipped away except the desire to see his father. He didn't slow, even as the gates of the village came into view and the guards shouted at him, demanding an explanation. The gates were opened and he ran straight into his father's courtyard, collapsing as soon as the main door came into view.

"Lord Sehouma!"

"My father," he croaked, uncaring of the strange looks he was getting as the servants flitted around him. "Get my father."

The murmurs intensified as they tried to pull him to his feet and take Kay's limp form from him, but he growled and curled further around her.

"My father," he said again. "I need my father."

"Fetch Lord Kouran," the servant kneeling before him said, and Sehouma finally heard someone rush off to fetch him. He refused to relax his protective stance over Kay even as the footsteps returned and his father's trademark white clothing filled his vision.

"Please," he whimpered as his father knelt before him, his voice cracking with exhaustion. "Please heal her."

Kouran glanced briefly down at the girl in his arms before locking eyes with him once more.

"What is the meaning of this? Why have you abandoned your post?"

Sehouma shook his head, feeling his strength wane. "Please, just heal her. Then I will explain, I promise." He was having trouble holding his eyes open as he gazed up at his father, who had risen to his feet and was returning to the house. "Please father."

The older man turned back to face him, anger burning in his eyes, and Sehouma feared all had been for nothing. But then, his father gave the tiniest of nods and it was all he could do not to collapse with relief.

"Very well, let her go and I will do what I can."

Sehouma shook his head again, refusing to release the girl even when more servants appeared to pull her from him. "Not here. Her arm is broken. Too harsh here."

"Sehouma!" Kouran replied harshly. "You can barely stand. Let her go now before you collapse atop her."

He fought the urge to challenge his father and hesitantly set her on the cold flagstones, his legs shaking as they fought to keep him upright.

"You are a fool," his father chided as he knelt over the girl. "Her injuries would have healed on their own. And yet you ran her all the way here, non-stop by the looks of it. You have abandoned your post and almost killed yourself over a silly girl. Have I taught you nothing?"

"I couldn't....couldn't leave her," Sehouma wheezed, his body now adamantly fighting sleep. "I...I think I love her, father."

If he hadn't been looking, Sehouma would have missed the slight widening of his father's eyes. A second later, Kouran turned his gazed once more upon Kay, who was now moaning in discomfort. He raised his hands over her, and as Sehouma's exhaustion consumed him, he saw his father's aura rain over the girl and heard her soft sigh as her bones mended.

Chapter Fourteen

Sehouma jerked awake, wondering how long he'd been asleep. He was in his own bedroom, which surprised him, but then again he could hardly expect his father to leave him sleeping in the courtyard.

"The fool awakens."

Sehouma jerked towards the voice. "Where's Kay?" He said, unnerved that he hadn't sensed his father seated by the fire. He tried to push himself up, but his arms shook with the effort and he collapsed back into the blankets.

"Asleep. I might have been able to heal her wounds, but she went two days with no food or water. She's weak. Why did you bring her here? How did this happen?"

His father watched him with guarded eyes, his arms crossed defiantly over his chest Anger rolled off him in waves, and Sehouma suddenly wished he'd remained asleep. But his father needed to know about the visitors. He'd failed in his job as protector, and now it was time to own up to it. "There are strangers in the forest." He said dejectedly. "They came on a ship. I have been trying to find a way to make them leave, but all possible options seem to lead to war."

"What does that have to do with her?"

"She came on their ship, but she is not their ally." He said the last part quickly, feeling his father's aura darken further. He had to make him understand. "She set up a camp where she could clearly watch them and has been living in the forest on her own since they arrived. However, two of the men attacked her. I heard her scream and arrived to find them preparing to violate her."

Kouran's eyes squinted in disgust. "Humans can be such vile creatures. You dealt with them I assume?"

"I killed one." He looked away, unable to face his father's disappointment any longer. "I'm sorry father. I let my concern for Kay overwhelm my senses. I didn't think."

Kouran snorted. "That much is obvious. All that remains now is to fix the problem. How many men are there? Has the Elder been discovered?"

"Not yet," Sehouma replied, shaking his head. "But there have been several close calls. I just can't think of a solution. If I kill them, scouts from their land will no doubt be sent in search of them. If I do nothing, it is only a matter of time before the Elder is found."

"I see."

"I'm sorry father."

"Stop apologizing boy. I said we would take care of it. For now, rest."

He left, closing the door behind him, and Sehouma felt his vision waver as he slipped back to sleep. In his dream, Gaasyendietha, the mythical dragon that guarded his family's temple in the Great Lakes, granted him the gift of flight, and he was able to carry Kay home atop a giant white cloud.

When he awoke, Sehouma scoffed. The dragon was no more likely to grant him the power of flight than to fly Kay home himself. No; he was on his own with this one. He had failed as a protector and as a son. His father's expression when he'd seen him in the courtyard had been proof of that. He just hoped he could redeem himself by miraculously figuring out a solution.

Chapter Fifteen

Kay jerked, her entire body tensing as she returned to consciousness. The last thing she remembered was falling out of the tree. Immediately reaching for her arm, she frowned as she wiggled her fingers easily. She could have sworn she'd broken her arm when she fell, but she felt no pain – although her arm shook with the effort to hold it aloft. Taking mental notes on her surroundings, she assessed the situation. She was definitely in a bed, and as far as she could tell, she was not on the ship – a good sign she hoped. She tried to sit up, but a towering weariness overwhelmed her, and she collapsed back into her bedding.

"Easy there,"

She jerked again, finally noticing the plump woman stoking the fire. "Wh-who are you?"

"Fret not child," she replied warmly, dusting off her hands and standing to face her. "You're in no danger here. My name is Haida. Lord Kouran asked me to look after you."

"Lord Kouran?"

The older woman nodded. "You've had quite the adventure. Do you remember what happened?"

Kay shook her head, which swam dangerously with the movement. "Where am I? How did I get here?"

"You are in Lord Kouran's home. Lord Sehouma brought you here."

"What? Sehouma is...a lord?" She rubbed her face, attempting to process this new information. Her friend was a lord? Then why had he been living in the forest?

"Yes, he's the Lord's eldest." Haida said, nodding as she reached over to place a gentle hand on her forehead. "I haven't seen him in years. It was quite a shock actually."

"Where is he?" She made to get up again, wincing as her arms gave out under her.

"He's resting, as you should be," Haida tutted, helping her into a more comfortable position. It reminded Kay of her mother, and she couldn't help but be comforted by the older woman's presence. "I'll fetch you some food."

She bowed and backed out of the room, leaving Kay to her curiosity. Forcing herself to sit up a little, she glanced around the meager room. In addition to the bed, only the fire, a chest, and a small table and chair occupied the space. However, simple as it was, she marveled its modernness. Logically she knew Sehouma must live somewhere, but she never would have expected something like this. The walls were made of smooth stone, which contrasted well with the dark wooden floor and ceiling. She could also see part of a woven rug sticking out from under her bed. *I guess I'm really no better than the sailors. Expecting the natives to live in hovels.*

Haida returned with a tray of food, causing Kay's stomach to rumble deeply. "I hope this is acceptable," she said, setting the tray on the bed and helping Kay sit up fully, once again moving the bedding to help support her weakened form. "I wasn't sure what you'd like."

Looking down, Kay had to restrain herself from devouring everything in sight. She hadn't realized how hungry she was until now and she found herself almost too hungry to eat anything, fearful how her stomach would react. Chancing one of the berries, she closed her eyes in bliss as the sweet fruit dissolved in her mouth. Haida chuckled and she felt her face flush with embarrassment. "Sorry. I just feel as if I haven't eaten in days."

"From what I understand, you haven't. Now, I'll leave you to enjoy your food. I'll have a bath prepared for you once you've finished."

"Thank you," Kay replied, knowing she would definitely like this woman. She was tempted to ask her more questions, but her hunger would not be ignored. So, she watched Haida once again nod and back from the room, before turning all her attention to the feast before her. "Answers later. Food now."

Chapter Sixteen

Sehouma had never been an anxious being. Confront the problem head on and typically it would go away. But as he stood staring at the doors of his father's study, Sehouma had to admit he wanted nothing more than to run straight back to the Elder and forget all this. Steeling his features, he hesitantly knocked, waiting until he heard his father's mumbled "enter" before he opened the door.

"Good morning father."

"Did you sleep well?" His father asked without looking up from his scroll.

"Yes. I wanted to speak with you regarding the situation with the Elder."

"I have already dispatched sentries to observe the situation. They will protect the tree while we determine a solution."

Sehouma nodded, having expected this answer. "Would you like me to go as well?"

"I never wished you to go in the first place." Kouran sighed and finally looked up. Sehouma was relieved to see his eyes had softened. His father's anger appeared to have dissipated. "If you wish to return that is your decision, but first we need a plan. You have knowledge of these visitors. We will need it."

"Of course,"

Kouran gestured to the seat across from him, and together they began going through all their options. An hour later, they had laid out a detailed map of the area, Sehouma explaining as much about the visitors as he could remember.

"Our best bet is to completely shield the Elder," Kouran said. "We've been working on this for a while now. If it were hidden, it would not require constant protection. The natives are expanding their villages as well, and given what we know about humans, I wouldn't doubt a war to be fast approaching should they meet these new visitors. Therefore, if we allow things to continue as they are, it is only a matter of time before the Elder Tree is discovered. We need a more permanent solution; one that doesn't require exiling one of our own to a lifetime of solitude."

Sehouma dropped his gaze to the floor. He hadn't realized how much work his father had put towards this. When he'd left home nearly fifty years ago, he hadn't intended to return, and he hadn't thought his father cared. Not after he'd basically refused the throne.

"I'm sorry for leaving," he said abruptly, cautiously glancing up at his father.

Kouran sighed, setting down the scroll before him to meet his son's gaze. "I was only trying to prepare you."

It was as close to an apology as he would get. Nonetheless, Sehouma appreciated it. His relationship with his father had always been strained, a constant battle of wills that left little time for bonding. He appreciated his father as a ruler. He was good for the people, but Sehouma hadn't needed a ruler. He'd needed a father.

"We need a barrier," Kouran said blandly, interrupting his thoughts. Sehouma looked up to find him standing, consulting the shelves of scrolls behind his desk.

"That takes time though. We'd need innumerable guards and lookouts to ensure we weren't interrupted."

His father waved him off, continuing to search through the tomes. "Guards I have. What we need is a mage. A powerful one." He pulled an extremely dusty scroll from the shelf and returned to the table, a confused Sehouma watching him intently.

Chapter Seventeen

Kay smiled, stretching like a cat under her bedding as she lazily returned to consciousness. Camping was fun, but nothing beat sleeping in an actual bed. It had been almost a week since she'd woken up in this room for the first time, and she was having trouble convincing herself she couldn't stay here forever. True, for the first few days she'd been here, she hadn't been able to do much more than lay in bed and talk to Haida, but as her strength returned, she'd been unable to resist exploring. Yesterday she'd spied what looked like a garden through a high tower window, and she was itching to find it.

She had to admit, part of her reason for exploring was her desire to speak to Sehouma again, but according to Haida, he was still spending most of his time either resting or stuck in his father's study. Apparently her friend hadn't stopped to rest the entire way here, too concerned with getting help for her. She felt honored, knowing he had taken the guardian post in order to escape home. She hoped he wasn't in too much trouble for bringing her here.

She wandered the halls aimlessly, completely lost to her thoughts until she turned a corner and almost ran into someone on the other side. Looking up, she gasped as she stared up at a man who could only be Sehouma's father. He was a little taller than her friend, and his hair was tied in a long plait down his back instead of loose, but otherwise he was an exact mirror image.

"I'm so sorry!" she said, bowing slightly in respect as she remembered Haida saying this was the man who had healed her. "Please, excuse me. I was not watching where I was going."

"There is no need for that," Kouran said, indicating she should rise. "Your injuries are no longer bothering you I hope."

"Uh, no." She murmured. "They're completely better. Thank you." He nodded, and Kay nervously looked at her feet, uncomfortably aware she was speaking to a king. When Haida had first explained Sehouma's lineage to her, she'd been baffled. Her friend just didn't seem like a noble – not that she'd met many nobles in her life. There was no denying it with this man though. His very aura exuded power and control. It was more than a little intimidating. He motioned down the hall and she followed him, unsure what she should say.

"I'm sorry," she blurted finally. It seemed only right; after all it was her fault Sehouma had abandoned his post.

Kouran paused, frowning down at her. "Whatever for?"

"Sehouma only came here because of me. It's my fault the Elder is unprotected."

Kouran's eyes widened slightly, and she wondered if he was surprised she knew of the Elder. He recovered quickly though, waving her off. "There is nothing to apologize for, my dear. We have already taken care of it."

She sighed, relieved. "That's good. I still feel bad though. How is Sehouma?"

"He's fine. He tells me you're an explorer."

Unbidden joy sparked within her at the thought of Sehouma discussing her with his father. Unsure why though, she brushed it off, trying to remember Kouran's question. "Exploring is in my blood, but this is my first actual expedition. My father arranged it for me."

"You must miss him."

He faltered, just for a moment, and Kay glanced towards him, surprised by the warmth of his gaze. Whatever issue had driven Sehouma to leave, there was no denying his father cared for him. She wondered how hard it had been for him to send away his son, knowing he might not ever see him again. Then again, hadn't her father done the same? Her heart sank, realizing she now had no way to contact her father. She couldn't risk getting near the ship to smuggle a letter to him.

"Oh good, you're here," Kouran said, pulling her from her thoughts. They had somehow made it to the kitchen without her realizing it. She felt her face flush as she caught sight of Sehouma seated at a low table, his eyes seeking hers.

"I believe I have found a solution to our problem," Kouran said, motioning for Kay to sit as well. "But first I must ask you a question, my dear. Would you like to return home?"

"Home?" Her eyebrows furrowing in confusion. "To England?"

He nodded. "There is a way."

Unable to form a response, Kay simply stared at him. How could he hope to return her to England? Did she even want to return? Sure, she missed her father and would love to see him again, but was she willing to return to the suffocating rules and societal standards? As far as she could tell, Sehouma's people didn't care what gender you were. If you had a skill for something, you used it. It was a refreshing way of existing, one that she was not sure she wanted to give up.

"Where are you going with this, father? How does this solve the problem with the Elder?" Sehouma appeared just as confused as she was. His expression mirrored hers as both of them looked to the older man for an explanation.

"There is record of a highly powerful mage across the sea. I had forgotten about it until you mentioned this girl's home. I believe the two locations are the same. A vessel is being prepared to journey there. I need you, Sehouma, to go and explain the situation and therefore, if this girl wishes to return home, she may accompany you."

Sehouma frowned. "Why me?"

Kouran smiled sadly. "My son, as much as it pleases me to see you again, I know your heart longs for freedom. Also, logically we need someone knowledgeable of the situation who can explain it accurately. Time is of the essence here. We have no room for miscommunications. The mage must know exactly what is needed in order to accurately assist."

Kay was still skeptical. "How can you be sure it's the same place?"

"I have lived for many years. And did my own fair share of traveling when I was younger. I met the mage during my travels in your land. An interesting bunch of humans I must say. I particularly enjoyed the game of jousting."

Kay's heart soared. She may not want to return home for good, but she couldn't pretend she hadn't been upset by the realization she might not ever hear from her father again.

"When?" Sehouma said, his expression unreadable.

"Three days. The ship is being stocked as we speak."

"Very well," Sehouma replied solemnly. "Three days it is."

Chapter Eighteen

Kay stared in awe at the massive ship before her – a ship filled with both men and women. Sehouma stood beside her, looking slightly uneasy. He'd agreed to come on this trip, but right now he looked like he wanted nothing more than to run back to the forest. "Nervous?" She asked quietly, grinning as he jerked slightly.

"I have never been on a ship."

"This is my second time. Hopefully this trip goes better than the last. I want to learn to sail, but I've never been allowed to learn."

"Haha, you shouldn't have that problem this time."

Kay spun around, bowing slightly towards Kouran, who was walking towards them. He once again waved off her show of respect, and instead handed her a sealed letter. "This is for your father." Her eyebrows crinkled in confusion, her father? But before she could say anything, Kouran continued. "I'm well aware you are not intending to stay with your father. This contains information on how to contact my allies in your land. Consider it a favor from one father to another. No parent should have to feel their child is lost forever."

He glanced at Sehouma, whose gaze had fallen to the ground. "May I have a word, my son?"

Sehouma's gaze jerked back up and he nodded, following Kouran a ways away. Kay hoped they would be able to reconcile. She could tell they loved each other, but there was also pain as well. And it was not easy repairing relationships filled with such pain.

A cheerful greeting pulled her from her thoughts, and she turned to see Haida trotting towards her. "Thank goodness!" she heaved, bending slightly as she caught her breath. "I was afraid I wouldn't make it." She took a moment to compose herself, then handed a large bag to Kay. "This is for you."

"What? You didn't have to..."

"It's the salve for your skin. I made a new batch when I heard you would be leaving. I was getting worried it wouldn't be ready in time. I almost missed you!"

"Oh Haida! Thank you!" She pulled the older woman into a hug, wishing they'd been able to get to know one another more. It had been nice having a woman to talk to who wasn't trying to force her ideals on you all the time.

"I also packed extra ingredients in case you need to make more. Sehouma can show you."

"Show what?" Sehouma replied, reappearing beside her. Not waiting for an answer, he motioned to the ship. "We should board. Father said the ship will soon depart."

Nodding, Kay gave Haida another hug, promising to visit when she returned.

"Your new adventure awaits," she replied. "Go find it."

Kay grinned, blinking back tears as she followed Sehouma up the ramp and onto the deck. Kouran stood watching as well and she gave him one final bow, grinning as he once again waved her off.

"Ready?" Sehouma asked quietly – making her wonder if he were ready himself. His body was tense with nervousness, but remembering her first few moments on the ship from England, she understood. Seeking to reassure him, she threaded her fingers into his. His expression morphed into one of shock as he stared baffled at their entwined hands.

"With you, always."

About the Author

Willow J Wolfe began writing almost twenty years ago. She got her start writing Inu-Yasha fan fiction in middle school and hasn't stopped since. Willow lives in the mountains of North Georgia and spends her time playing video games, reading, and deciding which crochet project to work on next.

She is currently working on her first novel The Lost Princess, and still writes and publishes fan fiction under the name "Dlat" on Dokuga.com whenever she can.